Bizarrest Blunts

By: Jamie Nichole

Dedicated to those with no filter.

Bizarrest Blunts is the final installment of Jamie Nichole's poetry trilogy centered on uninhibited self-expression. There will be no way down from here. Readers will find bizarre thinking at the highest of levels when reading the pages of Bizarrest Blunts. These pieces of poetry sizzle with risk taking. Beware, that as a reader, you will be delighted with cognitive whiplash during and long after the reading of this poetry collection. Buckle up and enjoy the Bizarrest ride you won't regret having taken.

Sue Me

Wish I never knew you
Trash smells bad inside and outside the bag
If you live beyond the border,
your tax is all the more sweeter

Watch me eat the most for dinner
Hear Cha-rese talk shit about Quinti-fa
Alex works for both genders
Bread tastes better when thinner

Mice roam all through the winter
Geese never swim deeper
Homemade strife is cheaper
My dad went bald last summer

Cherrie's twat is so much cheaper
Birds fly home every spring
Serious money lacks cold water
Furious winds need a new liver
Black actually made her look even fatter
Sarcasm is her daily dinner
Bón appetite

Plasma

It came from a beaver's mouth
Sinks below real anatomy
He told her not to spend that much
Chinese serve it for breakfast
Shirley Sue drives it into the river
Dick loving Kyle sneaks mom past the door
Creates the most rebellious children
Often prevents desired penetration
Sends home fleas for dinner
Makes me want to slap that ass
Wait until this hits the thread
Eating steak makes Fred feel bigger
Shows off the biggest chest of all
Leads the all the way lost people
Houses plain applesauce,
that ends up just underneath the start of a cheek
Pays a small amount of money
#side hustle

Take Down your Tree

It's now January 23rd
We've seen more than our fair share
of how Uncle Humbert takes his dumps
Toilet paper is his favorite number
No one really looks at what's actually wrong
Adding lights makes my month see nearer
He only wanted your phone number
You bent over and swore to pick better next time
Santa knows whose pants are bigger
Feliz Navidad

Homemade Hot Sauce

Came from Chicago
Sailed all the way to Santiago
Wound up on every unread magazine cover
Left the almonds out
Treated jalapeños better
Designated Diego to take the trash out
He wears a bandana when he goes out
Taylor went all in with Sandra's mom
Uncle Ben is her only friend
It takes time to understand
the lyrics of Diana Ross
My mom forgot to tickle me
Now I lay him down to sleep
Him/he

What The?

1, 2, 3, go
down on Aunt Sallie
Then, tape their mouth shut
Seal the whole
so, everyone knows
how bad he sucks

My Face

Look me in the eye
Tell me your prickly white lie
My face knows the truth you choose to ignore
He stepped out on you for sure
He's always been the kind
who looks up every skirt
My face wears half of my abuse
Abusers would like to feel better
Instead of getting well,
they violate even the most well-guarded heart
My face needs a little help when you're around
Blushing, crushing, shushing, flushing me out
Say something really funny
This look should be my go-to face
It will land me tones of dates
That will never make it home
to meet mom and dad

Corn that Doesn't Digest

The trusted Heimlich won't work unless you fart
Best not to walk directly behind all the cars
Taller doesn't necessarily mean better
Long hair will never make your boobs bigger
Drinking cups of Zen tea
speeds your metabolism
Dogs don't know how to climb a tree
Chewbacca sheds when lying in bed
Making decisions comes with a few butt pimples
The bed shouldn't fit more than two
Hope comes when faith has been renewed
That step was more than obvious
Slice the ham when you think you can't

H-Bomb

H-VAC
HQ
CPAP
HEP C
HEP B
DTAP
Jock strap
Booby trap
Catnap
Q-tip
You know it's not me
Flu A
Flu B
Honolulu
Preparation H

Finger Licking Bad

Disease in your nads
came from playing hopscotch
with your boss's wife

Disease in your female anatomy
came from saddling up one too many times
with foreign objects lying around the house

Disease in your mind of minds
came from swinging lie to lie
with zero ability to believe in the truth

Disease in your heart of hearts
came from always being misunderstood
with little to no recourse from the sourest
sinking of souls

Hold the Fart

When the prayer is being prayed
When you're in the elevator
When you're having your prostate exam
When you're tying your shoes
When your new girlfriend is walking behind you
When you're doing yoga in public
When grandma is beside you
When the wind is blowing south
When you're pledging the allegiance
When you're wearing thin pants
When you're pulling up the weeds
When you're walking down the aisle
When you're driving with no air conditioning
When you just ate refried beans
When sitting pretty in the tub
When they're singing happy birthday
Even when you think you can't

Release the Fart

When you're sitting next to your worst enemy
When you're driving by a skunk smell
When the chair is old and gray
When you're running in the rain
When they love you anyway
When the song is loud enough
When the toilet is beneath you
When the hallway is dark
When the chicken was fried
When the dog passes gas first
When your underwear is already dirty
When Santa brings you coal
When you sneeze with force
When the store is Walmart
When the avocado is not ripe
When you want to blow them away
Every stinking time they were right

Penis Ring

How many dings have you donged?
Does it feel nice going into the black deep?
What makes you need to pee?
Should you brag about working in threes?
When will your foreskin actually fall off?
Didn't you already ring that bell?
Can't you rest your stick one year?
Will you be ok,
when the blood doesn't flow anymore?
How big is your diamond?
May we take a tiny peek?
Do you prefer to think it's super rare?
Why is there so much green hair?
How often do you itch?
Is it alright if you bend all directions?
What's the last good smell you've smelled?
May I have a lil bite?
Please slap me on both sides.

Friends with Bitches

If your friend is nothing but a snitch,
do they at least know extra bitches?

Extra bitches might be worth the lost device
Wing men are supposed to know when to step in

Most of the time,
they want the catch for themselves
Choose your friends loosely

Cling to the upright tightly
Go home when they can't act right

When they take your moves,
tap their chin gently
When they do it again, slap their face loudly

If you really want to meet your queen,
stop trying to find her arbitrarily

Bet

Chicken Dinner

I want something plain and trite
I want something that once gawked gibberish
I want to fry that which I can't deny
I want to eat wings that no longer fly
I want to eat something
that can no longer reproduce
I want to chomp on white meat with cut off feet
I want to make certain
the barbeque sauce gets used
I want to dip my food in liquid msg
I want to consume
cubes and strips of broken blood vessels
I want to burn my husband's
favorite dish on purpose
I want to choke
on thick boiled pieces of bird flesh
I want to eat a protein source
that is good left over
I want to eat the Thanksgiving reject
I want to pull out all the innards
I want to use a rotisserie
from the store as an original dish
I want to eat my cat's entrée of daily choice
I want my digestive system cranking solids
Too bad you're not the winner-winner

In Tune

Forget what happened before
Look at all the good in store
Find the gems in the puddles you create
Take away the strings that didn't belong
Twist the knobs that control the theme song
Test the deep unknown waters without floaties
Adjust the position of your moral compass
Walk toward the sounds that soothe
Be willing to be played more than one way
Losing sight of you is how you got out of tune

Mature Trees

Know that love matters most
Grow in non-toxic soils
Swim in both the shallow and the deep
Need little external celebrity
Make the most of animosity
Take the sun in on both sides
Lose old leaves lacking true positivity
Don't care how tall they are
Trust without concrete certainty
Are ok with not getting to drink all the water
Dream of permanent roots
Choose to forgive without an apology
Treat others with undeserved dignity
Laugh when they've had more than one can take
Sleep ready for more adversity
Chase down every kind opportunity
Wish everyone's needs were always met
Avoid other trees with unholy rot
Stand strong in the face of the storm
Grow in all possible directions
Need time to become ready to bear good fruit
Kiss the wind that is their enemy
Deserve to be seen
Find comfort under mature trees only
Other trees just keep failing their seasonal tests

Sintopia

You want utopia?
Face your feartopia
Hop over your large gestationaltopia
Prick open your corrupt vasculartopia
Swap places with your cerebraltopia
Take the next plane to Santiago
Rip off her dress like it's going sour
Lie silver slushes into Theresa's unmade bed
Tie a knot for your grandma to chew
Pull Sénior Sam out from your underpants
Go five over the speed limit
Pay Uncle Sam less than you can
Fly the proverbial broom
Sit in everyone else's sloth
Take less than one bite
Friend every guy in the room
Wear a backward woman's dress
Slay the innocent in the room
Go to Hell

Artificial Air Freshener

Burns your momma's tenth grandson
Finds a bed in your nostril hairs
Sizzles on the tongue for days
Activates sexual activity blockers
Dries wet on all types of floors
Chases every guy named Lightening McDream
Poses as what usually last an hour
Takes the rispy right out of the crispy
Sends me to aisle three for butt cream
Gives my deodorant a hump in the shower
Withers the fake leaves
Flies nude into your coffee cup
Tricks him into being with ugly Pam
Is cheap for a toxic reason
We are so sick of snorting Hawaiian Breeze

My Mom's Boss

He lost the war
He phoned it in
He tripped on Tom's thumb
She left her Groupon at home
She drank so he could keep up
She laughed into his ass

Math

Makes me mad
Pulls out my nose hairs one by one
Drives me over the limit to the bakery
Leaves my bank account empty
Incites tears from my asshole
Is to blame for every annoying
speed bump on the planet
Will never be one size fits all
Takes the cake out of the fun
Requires counting machines
Pours me the tallest long island
Makes zero cents

Today is Better

Summer fries never-ending,
connecting all the people
Here comes September
Forget her magic number
Open up to November
He always drank all the liquor
Give me up come December
Drop me like a New Year kombucha
Change my life every January
Caress my heart into
unconditional February love,
that transcends past March allergies
Buy me every new Apple product in April
Swing past all that comes whatever in May
Junipers travel faster than Winter
Sexually transmitted disease is boiled in July
Augusta never was a good mother

No Way Rosé

You went the wrong way two days in a row
Don't drive past what makes you fat
Question if she's here to stay
What gives the suggestive apple sauce?
How much pubic hair did the dog ingest?
Just when will you ride better than that?
That is your absolute best dressed?
Isn't the right boob bigger than the left?
Who cares what Aunt Tina ate in bed?
My grandma's nose has smelled a lot less dread
Can we sip unyoked alabaster?
I will be your dry humored designated driver
Make it home before the final falter
Seek revenge in the up-hand position

You Guyz

Want to share cold eyes?
My peace I won't bestow
So, lean on low mileage wind instead
Send Italian emojis
Bring politics up before cheers
Keep fake believing you're a good friend
Eat karma boiled on a medium
Relax yourself into mental veneers
Shy away from calculated maneuvers
Take the bacon home to momma
Punch my butt when you recall trauma
Smell my face when the coast is clear
Never leave a verbal bib on her
Très exuberance
I want to know who cries inside their tooth
Let's try to never forget
this moment
when we saw
in between
her thighs
just
let
me
die

Almost Humane

It can't speak faster than prime rib
There should be some more of bliss
Take a quick look between my toes
Sweep it past genres that don't mention ass
Over price the advice asked twice
Slide home to what you never knew
Take down stained underwear
Treat rice with every grain
Bet you laughed yourself insane
It's time you moved out of her drool
Leave mammoths up to God
Find home where you don't belong

Name The Car

Open up the drawer
Put on what can never be lost
Drink more than the speed limit
Waste how you first tied your shoes
Create funnels of how I lost my job
Tear down ordinary dreams
Post my best every now and then
Thank the one who walked in last
How many times shall I resend?
We've reached the bitter end

Who's Santiago's Boss?

There is this man you will regret to transgress
His ball carriage is more than unforgiving
She ripped his crinkled pant suit
off his chicken legs
He can't divide his own fractions
Intense blue balls tend to distract him
It's not like he always wants to scream
She left him for a more
productive testosterone hog
He kept slapping the wrong tush
You definitely should go knee deep,
if you desire to make more

Alarm Clocks

Send illiterate shocks-
to grown-up flocks,
of lowly cunts on the rocks
Grant him re-entry
Allow all things in
Last three fourths of the time
How can we snooze having drank all the booze?
Take me high in a black air balloon
Never look at her again
Digital timers repent more than others
Find more conceptional options,
because tomorrow is never promised

Pin the Tail on Your Trauma

What burns the most self-delusions?
Understand what results in living suicide
Your vintage purse didn't erase the hurt
You eat what is burnt
The last time you felt special,
hell was frozen over
Situations are never ending
We spent more than we had
Our parents are still alive
Grandma left your mother with splinters
It's easier to cook your own dinner
Traumatized is your whole existence

I'm That Kinda Friend

That eats your gross leftovers
That dreams we were queer
That wears a dirty thong
That finds all the good bars
That excitedly switches it up every now and then
That buys with never trying on
That wears daily black eyes
That waits until later
That gets us deeper in the hole
That sleeps with almost family
That drinks while they chew
That streams hate within
Wanna be my only friend?

You Can't Rent Two Dildos

Two is not better than one,
when you can simply use your thumb

Break her in half with one hand
Land on moley skin that scolds once a month

One pays less rent to go down south,
but she can lift her own somewhat heavy shit

Dads try to bestow holy daughters
Girls turn into women
who ride the wave of sorrow

Light between their thighs brings laughter
One woman holds enough man power

Pay Your Rent

Say I'm sorry
Clean their mess
Fold their beer
Tell them how good they make you feel
Wipe up their suicide
Tie their shoes at night
Cry when they don't come home
Be glad he didn't over slap you
Let the window down and flip them off
Grow through what you did to them
Send gifts with violins
Share why you forget every single time
Drive the carpool that starts at 6:00 am
Lose weight that changes your face
Present bilingual artifacts
Shake down moments after the disaster
You will always need more green friends

Take A Seat

Please sit next to me
I am willing to smell your feet
We do better in threes
Don't skip over me
Make long term eye contact with me
Our connection will make you sing
Don't run up that dead oak tree
The bark shows tons of scars
Next to me, is just where you ought to be,
forever next to me

Waiting at the DMV

Nothing compares to a trip to the DMV
If you see me headed there,
please feel sorry for me

At the DMV, there is plenty to see
There you will find every ethnicity,
all in the same room
Some folks come dressed in their pajamas

The best show stars an angry momma
Even with an appointment,
you will wait two to three hours

If you're lucky, you will sit or stand next to
someone who doesn't stink
The ones who took a bath,
will leave unhappy as can be

Workers work slow on purpose
Why can't we upload a selfie instead of listening
to fugly babies cry?

Should We?

Jump off this dangerous cliff?
Drive our car into the beach?
Play our cards absolutely straight?
Take Mikey home for good?
Send Rhonda back to school?
Pray to God?

In The Kitchen

It's where we combine for wine
It's where we smell what's coming
It's where our phones have intermission
It's where we release inhibitions
It's where we taste past decisions
It's where we pray for non-believers
It's where grandma releases secrets
It's where mom poisons dad
It's where we consolidate grand visions
It's where we salt old wounds
It's where black and white collide
It's where oil makes everything better
It's where France invades bread
It's where Einstein made his one bad decision
It's where milk settles bellies
It's where the lights never go off

My Mom Knows

I turned three
I do not eat bananas
I die to self
I wish for more sincerity
I could kill myself
I want to see this through
How about you?

Goodnight

Teddy is in bed with Freddy
Both ate Salmon and rice
Only one's breath smells half-way nice
Backs are braised for ugly names
Shoulders are raised just incase
Teddy hits Freddy
Freddy likes it
They will always be best friends for life
Both fall asleep sucking each other's thumb

Zip Me Up

I like to fly with my fly open
The air massages every part of me
There's not much for you to see
I like to leave the conversation open
The air otherwise catches my tongue
I like elephants in the room
The air smells mysterious when trunks are open
I like dripping butter everywhere I go
The air tastes better
when sprinkled in body margarine
I like exposing myself to the trees
The air is out to get the best of me

Jesus Freaks

Pay their own bills
Keep it above the belt
Stand for peace
Fight the east and the west
Believe in a holy mess
Stare at evil on purpose
Love blindly
Treat people kindly
Avoid trouble
Respect their parents
Throw rocks at Lucifer

Dating Kirkland

I love how affordable you are
Buying bulk gets my gears going
You have the best low-cost champagne in town
I like how you are willing to work on my car
while I walk your aisles
Your grocery carts are the biggest around
The meat you're packing is fresh, thick, and
salted in decadent affordability
When Covid hit,
you helped me keep wiping my butt
It's amazing how people come to you
to buy shit they don't need
Just one hang up though,
why must I pay to play in your club?

Trading Up

Means he won't take it out on you
Shows you truly can do better
Takes making prior mistakes
Never makes the grass greener
Happens after fifty feral dinners
Lives under good weather
Tickles unfinished business
Is the goal when you let them go
Hears the non-committal laughter
Saves the best for last
Rips the rug out from under forgotten love
Wipes its feet with their insecurity
Leaves the clothes on generosity
Drives me home to dad

Thanks

For endless pounds of cheese
I would do anything
I would jump from the tallest tower
I would dance and sing
Yell it from the tallest mountain
Scabby cheese
Scab
Scab
Scabby Cheese
I put that scabby cheese on everything-
from cereal to smores
People think I'm crazy, but they're only looking
in the mirror
Am I right?
Am I?
Am I?
The cheese is just out of reach,
but I'd rather have the squeeze
of orange and red obscenity
and hot and pulsing scabby cheese
Oh cheese, you do it for me
Why is it that you control me?
For I am now Queen Scabby
and the cheese is upon you
Here's the best cheer your step dad holds near
Oh, blessed scabby cheese

Record Breaking

Sex
Sleep
Sailing
Singing
Stringing
Streaming
Speeding
Sounds

Fish and Brits

Take fat girls out to dinner
Save the date the flowers expire
Read between the tea hours
Find trees to be a bother
Grow up smoking jail
Take toll primarily in winter
Steer past celibacy
Cause trouble with Grant's mother
Rectify thin lines
Pray every legal day
Leave you feeling dark
Quit right after they get paid
Stir deep inside
Greek me
Twice

Selective Sara

Pulled down my underwear
Drove past every flat chest
Left me at Applebee's
Drank serenaded falafels
Slept with more than ten short men
Opened up every can of worms
Slapped me all the way home that night
Creamed more than she could scream
Flew back to where I left her
Smelled better than Alabama plaster
Tries every knew scent
Hears only what she listens to
Covers up her tracks
Believes she'll never have to pay it back
Can't see her life in black and white

Follow Me

I'll see you through haunted streets
I'll see you beyond your poor genetics
I'll see you when karma loses fame
I'll see you when nobody harms themselves
I'll see you when the speed limit is the same
I'll see you before dimples occur
I'll see you when my vagina feels like it
I'll see you when he swallows all the pills
We will no longer have to fight his fiery
We will walk in bended balls
We will see no hair color
We will own our sanity
We will pay what it costs
We will dive right in
We will smoke from the plant's ears
We will never worship bacon again

See Here

My life is almost over
I was a good lover
You could bargain on my French kiss
Never forget the privilege of the touch of my lips
Smell the fermented amber beer
She weighs less than the Almanac does
Cross over to lip stick lesbians
You'll see more chest than planned for
Homerun for every loyal biological son

Give a Flip

Right outta the fucking blue,
here comes you
This drives his mom insane
I will always pay you,
more than you pay me
Screw three trains instead of four
Hear her out before you eat her out
Stand on three trees then count to ten
Smell every beard that comes near
Shake hands with naughty types of beer
Wish her well,
then tell her to get on her knees
No one wanted her for who she is
She lives a life of shame with no name

The Sheets

Know almost everything
Experience your epidermis scent
Taste your aphrodisiac
Mispronounce your foreign last name
Drive all straight men insane
Wrap me up in crazy making disdain
Hold my every wet tear
Shelter my mind from fear
Answer the phone while drinking beer
Smell like savory butter popcorn

Step-believers

Got one foot in and one foot out
Hold in their stinky farts
Pretend to know the actual verse
Wish to God
Know better
Drink when Peter's asleep
Grab their own ass
Smell like an unpleasant Christmas dinner
Get scared when the light's not on
Always call their mom
Don't really want to bother
Make up more than half of the corporate Church
Really need a Jesus fix
Refuse a real Christmas tree
Slap the gnats on their freckled backs
Freak out when stuff runs out
Cry out for an unoriginal first name
Possess hearts with religious crystal darts
Sometimes forget to say amen
Drive Uncle Tom up the wall
Equally fall on their sinful bended knees

Jam Session

Spread thin
Wanna play
Ate all day
Drank Aunt Bae
Tapped that ass
Rocked Uncle Sam
Mistreated sweet Aunt Pam
No one ever understands,
why one plus one is a really small sum
Last time I checked,
my headache ain't my fault
Was a ruckus to begin
Peace out my dear old friend

High

See my kite up there?
Be careful, I might pull down your underwear
It's so high
I will need to say goodbye
If only my boobs sat that high
Why does God make the clouds cry?
Mow the grass before it dies
Being low makes you addicted to bubble gum

Tricks, but No Treats

Knock, knock
Who's there?
Was I supposed to care?
That is the worst way to comb your hair
Don't worry about why they stare
Hold hands until they start to sweat
Flip the table over their laps
Send one less than what they request
Let the fly in on purpose
Eat the first and last bite
Sing until it becomes a bad memory
Pretend you're not at home
Let them find out the hard way
Allow the door to close behind you
Say all the worst right to their face
Take over even when you're not first place
Serve them cheap shots of apple sauce
Enjoy fresh air while they connect the dots

Rainy Ways

Drip drops on my secret hot spot
The sun could never beam me up the way I want
Tigers look thinner wet, isn't that super great?
Sideways in the afternoon delight we go
Let my core flood with blessed acidity
I ripen in the absence of sunshine
Days mist the best kisses
from dark heavy clouds
There's no reason for suicide
just because it's gray outside
Umbrellas come in fifty million colors
Pick one and learn to listen to the cleansing
Every bad pickle needs an unexpected bath
Your hair might frizz, but it demonstrates life
The fragility within a single hair strand,
represents what can't be understood
Find solitude in the free space
between puddles of sinful buildup
Allow each rain drop
to nearly make your heart stop
In this sweet calm,
is breath in tune with the creator

Hell-o

Don't you see all the hypocrisy?
Don't you see all the tomfoolery?
Don't you see he spends all his green on green?
Don't you see that her hair
has been dyed 50 million times?
Don't you see everyone here
thinks you're absolutely annoying?
Don't you see that it's not always about you?
Don't you see why I will never trust you?
Don't you see friends are both good and bad?
Don't you see my words cut right through you?
Don't you see the world
will eventually come to an end?

They're Fired

I can't do this anymore
No one can make me want to
My heart is over it
I tried my freaking best
So, what's next?

Here we go again
I'm reluctantly back for more
Punch me in the face
I deserve a violent wake-up call
Maybe it will work this time

Third time's the charm
Yet, I'm having to twist my own arm
Start strong and fade in the middle
Grown up stuff tastes like dog kibble
Watch me double dribble trying not to ugly cry

Pubic Hair

Grows all over
Gets stuck in your throat
Keeps you from going the distance
Ends up on the toilet
Tells your dirtiest secrets
Hides how big you are
Provides cushion for pushing
Makes frail grandma throw up
Is why we call men chumps
Is invisible after a few drinks
Causes an unforgettable stink
Would hold in all the oatmeal
Winds up on the floor
Creates a daily chore
Ruins sex on the floor
Is why we close the door

Loud Laughs

Sometimes laughs are contagious
Those laughs don't need a chip clip
Laughter that raises an eyebrow,
should result in a friendly bitch slap
No one wants to have to cover their ears
Ears are meant to hear the sweetest sounds
Ears are not meant to frown
The bigger the humor, the quieter the laugh
Silent laughs bark the loudest
Boisterous laughs should rot in the hottest hell
Maria's tits jiggle when she laughs out loud
Dan's wiener shrivels when his wife snorts
Moms of more than one,
trickle laughter particles into their pants
Juan spits his food when he sees people trip
All laughs don't go to heaven

Dumb Donkey

You can't even count to three
Your mom applies your band-aids
Your dad throws the ball for you
The air brushes your hair
The rain cleans your stank away
The grass wipes your feet flippers
Other people laugh at your hairy perched ass
Other people spank you verbally
Other people think for you
Social media will never blow you
Social media doesn't replace real friends
Social media pays less than McDonalds
Time will surely tell
Time won't make you swell
Time was what you bought at a price
Facts are what you lack
Facts will pin you to the wall
Facts get in your way while they ruin the day
Now all you can do is try not to get shot
Now you're fatter than yesterday
Now we'll all watch your tail sway
He-haw, he-haw, he-haw

Yelling

Want to know how to demean?
Yell
Want to know how to ruin the fun?
Yell
Want to know how to break trust?
Yell
Want to know how to kill the love?
Yell
Want to know how to scare the meek?
Yell
Want to know why she killed herself?
Yell
Want to know all she heard as a child?
Yell
Want to look like the fool?
Yell
Want to lose their respect?
Yell
Want to be the douche?
Yell
Want to never see her again?
Yell

Thomas the Great

He owned the entire estate
He slept with anyone who would
He left his poop in the toilet
He felt inspired to wear two hats
He peed siting down
He wished he could play guitar
He tended to spill his beans
He spanked himself after every fart
He drank other people's tea
He never knew his Wi-Fi password
He wanted to remain three years old forever
He had zero dollars in his piggy bank
He missed every time he swung the bat
He kind of split his sack
He was obviously not all that

Santie Clause

Don't play with elevated blue contradictions
You'll get bent over the white moon
Listen closely to every single red word
If you expect to be heard, wear white seashells
Live vicariously through green pieces of paper
Read in between gray lines
Erase all the orange collateral
Highlight yellow indirect threats
Take obsolete purple hearts to task
Drop your hypothetical brown front
Sign slightly above the solid black line

Hippie Tree

Hug me
Rub me
Pet me
Taste me
Sniff me
Bite me
Fist bump me
Urinate on me
Forget to shave your pits for me
Spank me
Bump butts with me
Flash me
Tickle me
Drool on me
Nail me

Phony Bologna

Walk in the room with arms crossed
Wear a serious face to intimidate
Sport a wide gait nobody appreciates
Give disapproving looks as if we are crooks
Say too bad, so sad
Be less than impressed
Drop invisible sweat from your dress
Get a clue instead of more new shoes
Baby blue doesn't look good on you
Infusion of cucumber has led you to confusion
Whack is all I have left to say about you

This is Dumb

Can we move on?
We will never see eye to eye
We will never care about the same things
We will not find a common point
You are a dull minded soul
You are as shallow as they come
You are a closed worst selling book

Get Out or I Quit

Fuck you bitch
Who do you think pays for this shit?
I make doe by causing other people trauma
All you did was vote for Obama
I had to lie upstairs to finance this new chair
That's why you left me here
I hope you never look over here again
Here is where my leftover trauma lasts forever,
all thanks to you know who boo

Jack-o'-lantern

Ridiculous subject matter
Will always be a lost cause
Sends letter A all the way to Z
Trade beer for water
Seek space in creepy cognitive space
Take that smart relic look off your face
Allow sand to invade your personal space
Leave time to be vehemently understood
The Bible reads exactly how it should
Who cares if I only make it to first base?

That's It

The end is here
Everyone is chalk full of schmear
Her mouth exults Polynesian cornbread salad
He never felt so damn sweaty
She kind of homemade some spaghetti
He resents ever driving an old Chevy
She refuses to count beats
He likes it when they're fat
She hopes to never sweat the bed
He freaks out when he's lost
Time to tell homeless Ted to find his forever bed

Somebody Shoulda

Called first
Ate the yellow and orange Starburst
Shook off religious holidays
Sat upon food without thought
Lashed out at beauty for being the beast
Taken the trash out
Stopped at the light
Dropped a dope beat
Washed the stinky feet
Bit the bullet
Slapped him silly
Drowned the lizard
Changed their diaper
Put out the fire
Rapped in pig Latin
Swam naked in the spilled beer
Held the door open
Changed the toilet paper roll
Turned off the stove
Oh no

Overrated

Chop liver
Monsters under the bed
Steak eating dentures
Chin hair in Winter
Burritos for breakfast
Green grass
Matching twins
Cherries on top
Homemade ice cream
Domesticated housewives
Young drivers
Unlit cigars
Panhandling
Presents prior to Christmas
40th birthdays
Different flavored Twinkies
Electric bikes
Driving backwards at night
Gluten free bread
Fake bacon
Crying in front of the mirror
Not thinking for yourself

Migrainez

Pain that tremors for days
Pain that has no cure
Pain that stops you in your normal tracks
Pain that has nothing to do with
your momma's back

Debbie Doesn't Do Dallas

She never misses church or school
She goes to bed two days sober
She wears grandma panties for every occasion
She cleans her room while wearing a halo
She looks before she crosses the street
She always says no thank you
She leaves before things go completely sour
She reads her Bible religiously
She never ever speaks true profanity
She shares with ugly people
She thinks before she thinks
She maintains her waist size
She has never tasted pale beer
She understands the need for slang
She makes everything homemade
She dreams about CBD lolli pops
She repents for others weak faith
She pays it forward
She lends instead of borrows
She laughs when they aren't funny
She doesn't exist

Clucking Bees

Swing on trees
Swarm the fruitful
Slap the wind
Sing subtle lies
String the flowers on
Slurp yellow thongs
See beneath the honey
Say I'll be back for more
Sting behind the knees
Strip on green stems
Savor what's left behind

Dark December

Dormant grass
Dormant hall pass
Dormant iced coffee
Dormant naps
Dormant open toes
Dormant lemonade
Dormant sunny music
Dormant neon stares
Dormant six packs
Dormant flies
Dormant sangria
Dormant clean streets
Dormant open windows
Dormant fold out chairs
Dormant sweaty underwear
Dormant lazy rivers
Living proof another year will have to unfold

What's Left?

There are chips, but no more dip
There is beer, but it isn't cold
There is cereal, but we don't have milk
There is shampoo, but we need more conditioner
There is a fire, but we ate all the marshmallows
There is plenty of paper,
but we're fresh out of ink
There is still school, but no one wants to go
There is a car in the drive way,
but all the lights are off
There are unending tears, but no tissue
There is definitely a toilet,
but it doesn't flush properly
There are billions of people,
but none of them truly believe
There is soap, but it doesn't want to foam
There is no macaroni, but we have some broccoli
There is a loaded gun, but they refuse to pull the
trigger

Clocking Out

Hip, hip hooray
I get to leave
Watch me come alive
I've never been happier to see my car
Time to go home and strum the guitar
Once we leave work, the happier we all are
Perhaps find a walk
Perhaps refuse to talk
Perhaps gorge yourself
Perhaps relieve yourself
Perhaps indulge in the fruit of your labor
Perhaps fall asleep on the couch
Rinse and remorsefully repeat
Reluctantly clock back in after little to no sleep

Eye T.V.

Watch the spider crawl up the wall
Watch the monkey swing on trees
Watch the butterfly swim in the air
Watch the rain drops make puddles
Watch the clouds stand still
Watch the leaves fall dead
Watch the bird peck the ground
Watch the light turn green
Watch the moth flirt with light
Watch the weeds tease the grass
Watch laughter fill the room
Watch friends walking hand in hand
Watch puppy love come to an abrupt end
Watch the water as it boils
Watch the toddler stomp their foot
Watch the fog fade away
Watch the lightening flash fear
Watch them take their last breath

NY Bites

Dirty streets with nonstop feet
The air whirling through tall buildings
Lies, smoke, trash, and feces are usuals scents
Nobody wants to speak, but the message is clear
Allure beyond complete recognition
Dreams of monkeys eating every banana peel
Lingerie window scapes
Noses to the Park Ave sky
Cussing fights right before your eyes
Posh dinners for you ought to know who
Eating pizza on the go
Crossing endless connecting streets
Horns to hear all the wrongs
Parks to infiltrate peace
Homeless prayers to subway heat
Come to see if you do or don't belong

Garbage

Stinks
Leaks
Trails
Yells
Moves
Grows
Rips
Slips
Weeps
Sucks
Mucks
Wishes
Laughs
Sleeps
Piles
Pretends
Promises
Forever

Abuse

It happens every day
to those big and small
to young and old
Abuse goes in and stays
Abuse stains the soul in serious ways
The abusers become the abused
The abused become the abusers
Self-love helps to start the healing,
but the love of the creator,
makes all things like new
Help the abuser and the abused
find the love they both need

In Between

Two people
Jobs
Lobster and crab
Jars of mayonnaise
French and sweet potato fries
Grandma's fat hands
Wet and dry boogers
Tight and baggy jeans
Santa's double chin
White and cheddar cheese
39 and 40
My front teeth
Who she thinks I am
Black and white
Passing out and puking
Slabs of Spam

Gray Glory

Took over the remaining active hair follicles
Cheers for others of all blood types
Let's lil fingers leave dirty smudges
Forgives and never holds a grudge
Stalks unchartered territory
Rises to the occasion when their parents are
stuck under drunk covers
Makes sure you never go hungry
Grows in beds of no longer fertile roses
Bears thorns of life long unspoken satisfaction

Happy and Fat in Action

Waddling willingly
Sulking sweet satisfaction
Living lies limitlessly
Trying truly to translate trauma
Picking problems prematurely
Mimics mysterious migration
Hears hallelujah hormones
Veers violently vanilla
Cares cruising comfortably
Drive drugs dumb

Camping

Is mostly free
Is when you don't take a shower
Is when you hug all the trees
Is when you sleep with all the bugs
Is when you burn the wilted wood
Is when you smell like smoke and dogs
Is when you get lost in unencumbered thoughts
Is when you kiss by a fire
Is when it rains on everyone's parade
Is when no one cares who's in charge
Is when you stop sucking your thumb
Is when you don't want to go into labor
Is when you have raw types of fun
Is when life comes to terms
Is when you smoke in secret, but your kids see
you through the trees
Is when laughter runs together
Is when flames smolder
Is when junk food is all food
Is when quiet runs uninterrupted
Is when dirt enters all crevices
Is when you sing to the night
Is when a beer is ok anytime
Is when adults have a sleepover
Is when everything is all right
Is when nothing is what must be done

Is when you eat ramen to be healthy
Is when one piece of fruit equals all
recommended daily servings
Is when lazy parenting makes you a good mom
Is when kids practice their survival skills
Is when we fantasize that we could actually
endure a zombie apocalypse
Is when a friend's poetry makes sense
Is when small dogs are queens
Is when nobody actually catches fish
Is when you pretend you heard it the first time

Tired of Your BS

You don't give a fuck,
about no one but yourself

Here's the simple answer,
my butt laughs long after

Your mustache hunts me
in the mystic shower

I wish he knew drunken matters
He wishes I knew what spiritually matters

Stars

They burst unconditional love
A love of exponential unreachable flickers
Emit odors of wrong and right remembered
Make the mistake of forgiving
the month of December
Sometimes lack respect for distant non-believers

My Boo

His smile makes me laugh
the kind of laugh that slaps cures
He intrigues in such a way
I can't figure out if he loves me too
He takes the cake when evaluating use of time
When spent with him, it is
the softest, surrealist, type of sublime

Static

Electricity
Neutrality
Specificity
Tranquility
Sensuality
Royalty
Homeostasis

Twisted Sisters

Eat a lot of tuna fish sandwiches
Repeat 1, 2, 3
Get drunk on ecstasy
Reap vaginal unpleasantries
Walk a mile to never been licked territories
Lift one saggy breast at a time
Rot their own vagina off

Douche Bag

You know them by their dry fruit
Never take a douche bag home
to meet your mom
He would rather take you straight to their
marshmallow bed
Listen to their actions twice,
or you'll end up the one not playing nice
They talk the pants off Aunt Jemima
which leaves her wishing
she left her syrup contained,
restrained, and with something left
to her ridiculous name

Stinky loser guys hang people out to cry
Take a look around
before they creep and crawl into
Mrs. Baird's underwear
that is filled with gluten yeast
that starts to wreak as bad as his webbed feet

Fall once, but not twice
Otherwise, you will be the butt of the ball
His own mom let him cry it out in the hall
That's where he escalated into the douche bag
you wish you never knew

That's So Not True

The moon has pubic hair
The cat got your tongue
My great grandma wears a thong
Love completely changes you
Confession humbles you
Frogs have retractable tongues
Grass tastes like frosted chlorophyll
The treason came without reason
Kids always honor you
Winter comes right on time
You won't regret it
There's no other way to say it
Old McDonald had a farm
I dance better when a Beyoncé song is on
Fish don't have feelings
My pecker is bigger than yours
Tricks are for kids
Walmart is cheaper than Target
The tooth fairy swallows your teeth
Traps always have at least one way out
High definition makes things clearer
I have nothing more to say

It has been my pleasure, to be a wounded vessel. For in this pleasure, I release the filthy poison to become laughter that falls into a nonsense river. Please never quiver at deep depths of cynical pepper.

Special thanks to friendly collaborators who joined the bizarre ride that is "Thanks" and "Camping." You know who you are.